haunted house!

Hang your coat
in the closet,
and I'll give you
a tour of my
haunted house.

This is the living room.

Would you like to sit on the sofa?

Or maybe you'd rather warm your toes by this roaring fire.

The dining room table
is set for our feast.

Down here is the cellar.

Be careful— it's dark!

Would you like to peek into this cupboard?

Now up to my bedroom. Hey!
Who's been sleeping in my bed??!!

How about a warm bath
before dinner?

This is the attic.

Aren't these
spider webs cute?

Let's see what's inside this old trunk.

Oh, dear!
Why are you
running away?